heartbeat

SHARON CREECH

heartbeat

SCHOLASTIC INC.

New York Toronto London Auckland Sydney
Mexico City New Delhi Hong Kong Buenos Aires

ISBN   0-439-76400-9

12 11 10 9 8 7 6 5 4 3 2 1   5 6 7 8 9 10/0

Printed in the U.S.A.   23

First Scholastic printing, February 2005

Typography by Alicia Mikles

for my bella granddaughter
Pearl Bella Benjamin
and
for my bello friend
William C. Morris

heartbeat

FOOTFALLS

Thump-thump, thump-thump
bare feet hitting the grass
as I run run run
in the air and like the air
weaving through the trees
skimming over the ground

touching down
thump-thump, thump-thump
here and there
there and here
in the soft damp grass

thump-thump, thump-thump
knowing I could fly fly fly
but letting my feet
thump-thump, thump-thump

touch the earth

at least for now ...

MAX

Sometimes when I am running
a boy appears
like my sideways shadow
from the trees he emerges
running
falling into *thump-thump* steps
beside me.

Hey, Annie, he says
and I say, *Hey, Max*
and we run
fast
and
smooth
and
easy
and we do not talk
until we reach the park
and the red bench
where we rest.

Max is a strange boy
thirteen
a year older than I am
deeply serious
determined.

He's in training
he says
in training to escape.

BEFORE I WAS BORN

My mother says
I was running running running
inside her before I was even born.
She could feel my legs whirling
thump-thump, thump-thump
and she says that when I was born
I came out with my legs racing
as if I would take off
right then, right there
and dash straight out of her life.

She says it made her laugh
and it scared her, too,
because she'd only just met me
and didn't want me to race away
quite so soon.

She says I've been
running
running

running
ever since—or nearly ever since—

I ran before I crawled
I ran from dawn to dusk
And sometimes at night
she would see my legs still restless
as if I were running
in my sleep
through my dreams.

I tell her not to worry
that I will always come home
because that is where
I get my start.

QUEASY

I was worried about my mother
who started taking naps
and stopped eating
and threw up in the kitchen sink
and in the bathroom
and in the car

and I was pretty sure
she had a deadly disease
and she would shrivel into nothing
and she would die
and I would be alone
with my father
who would cry
and I would run run run

but I would have to come back

thump-thump
thump-thump

sooner or later.

BUT!

But! My mother did not die.
She does not have a deadly disease.

Instead she has a baby growing
inside her
little tiny cells
multiplying every second

and the queasiness has stopped
and now she feels good—
like a goddess, she says

and we look at the books
which show cells
multiplying
and it seems miraculous
and strange
and sometimes creepy
and I ask her if it feels as if an alien
is inside her
and she says

Sometimes, yes.

GRANDPA

Grandpa lives with us
ever since Grandma died
and now we take care of him
because he is poorly.

He says he is falling to bits
little pieces stop working each day
and his brain is made
of scrambled eggs.

On his wall are photos
of when he was young
and he looks like me
with frizzy black hair
and long skinny legs
and often he is blurry
because he was running.

One photo shows him standing tall
with a medal around his neck
and a trophy in his hands
but his face is not smiling

and when I ask him why
he was not happy

sometimes he says:

I don't remember

and sometimes he says:

Is that me?

and sometimes he says:

I didn't want the trophy

and when I ask him why
he didn't want the trophy

sometimes he says:

I don't remember

and sometimes he says:

A trophy is a silly thing.

THE RACER

Mom says Grandpa was a champion racer.
He won the regionals when he was nine
and the state championship when he was twelve
and the nationals when he was fifteen
and then
he stopped
running

and he wouldn't say why

and he didn't run again
until my mother was three
and the two of them could run
together
and that, my grandfather told my mother,
was the only kind of running
he would ever do
because it was the best kind of running
and the only kind of running
that made any sense to him at all.

MOODY MAX

Moody Max
Moody Max
puzzles my brain.

I've known him all my life.
Our grandpas used to take us
to the same park
the one we run to now.

We balanced each other
on the teeter-totter
tossed sand at each other
dug in the dirt together.

We got older
played catch with pinecones
pushed each other on the swings
chased around the grass.

Max would laugh one minute
scowl the next

pinch my arm
and then kiss the pinch mark.

Then his father left
and his grandpa died
and Max got quieter
more serious
and when he ran
he pounded the dirt
with his feet
and ran farther and faster
as if he could run
right out of his life.

He thinks I'm spoiled
because I've got two parents
and a grandpa

and maybe he's right.

BARE FEET

We always run barefoot
Max and I
because we like the feel
of the ground
beneath us

gritty dirt
smooth leaves
crunchy twigs
polished pebbles.

Even when it's cold
we run on the hard, frozen path
our bare soles
slapping down.

Even when it snows
(which is hardly ever)
we fly through the wet fluff
our toes tingling

our feet red
and alive.

Some people think
we are a little bit crazy
running barefoot
through rain and mud and snow

but it doesn't feel crazy to us.

It feels like what we do

and it's one of the things
I like best about Max:
that he will run
barefoot
with me.

TICKETS

I am running up the path
behind the church
when my sideways shadow
Max
appears
falling into step beside me
thump-thump, thump-thump.

Hey, Annie

Hey, Max

and on we go round the bend
past four white birches
tall and thin
with leaves of gold
and peeling bark
like shreds of curled paper

and my breath is going out
into the air
into the trees
into the leaves
and his breath is going out
into the air
into the trees
into the leaves

and we breathe in
the air and the trees and the leaves

and we breathe in
our own breaths mixed together

and *thump-thump, thump-thump*
down the hill we go
to the creek

one l-e-a-p over to the bank

up the hill
past the old barn faded red
one side curved inward
like a big dimple

around the pasture
newly mown
smell of growing grass
slim green blades sticking
to our feet bare and brown

until we reach the red bench
beside the sycamore tree
with its mottled trunk
and wide yellow leaves

and we flop onto the bench
and breathe breathe breathe

while Max checks his time
on his grandpa's pocket watch
and he looks displeased

and says we will have to
pick up the pace on the way back

and I tell him
he can pick up his own pace
but my pace is fine
thank you very much

and he says I will never get anywhere
if I don't pick up my pace

and I tell him
I don't need to go anywhere

and he says
You might change your mind someday
and it will be too late.

He wiggles his feet
flexes his ankles
These feet are my tickets
out of here
he says

sounding tough
like a boy in a movie
not like the other Max I know.

I look at my feet
which don't look like tickets to me.
They look like two feet
browned by the sun
that like to run.

THE ALIEN

It is hard to believe
that the alien baby
is really growing inside my mother
because you cannot see anything
and she cannot feel anything—
not yet, she says—

and sometimes I dream
that it is not a human baby in there
but that it is a rabbit
or a mouse
or one time I dreamed it was
a miniature horse
silky and smooth
with petite hooves
and when it was born
my mother said
Oh! A horse!
It's not what I expected!

And I said we should keep it
anyway
even though it was not
what any of us expected

because it was rather a nice
little horse.

ROOMS

The baby is going to share my room
with me.
It is a small room but a crib will fit
and I am glad the baby
will be with me
although my mother says
it might be annoying at first
because the baby will wail and cry.

Grandpa says the baby should have
his room
that he should just get on with it
and kick the bucket
to make room for that baby

and my mother tells Grandpa
that he cannot kick the bucket
he is not allowed
because the alien baby
needs to see its grandpa

and sometimes Grandpa forgets
about the baby
and when my father bought
a pint-sized baby outfit
Grandpa said
Is someone having a baby?

And so we told him again
about the alien baby growing
in my mother
and Grandpa nodded
and said, again,
that he should kick the bucket
and make room for the baby.

I go out running
thump-thump, thump-thump
in the air, in the wind,
under the autumn sun
and I think about Grandpa

when he was young
running running running
and I wonder how it must feel
not to be able to run anymore
and not to remember even
that you could run once

and it seems as if
he is evaporating
or shrinking
disappearing—
little pieces vanishing each day

while the alien baby
grows bigger and bigger
multiplying cells
which I hope are baby cells
and not rabbit or mouse or horse cells.

MOTHER OF THE WORLD

We live in a small yellow house
on the edge of a small town
with one main street
and two stoplights.

Max lives in an apartment
not far from me.
He says he hates our town
and will live in a big city someday
where no one knows your business
and where there would be
a million opportunities
and even he—
"a small-town boy
without a father"
(which is the way he describes himself)—
even he could be somebody.

He gets mad when I tell him
he is already somebody.

Often he reminds me
that when I was seven
he asked me what I wanted to be
when I grew up
and my answer was
Mother of the World!
although I have no idea now
why I said that or what I meant.

Max said—at seven—
that he was going to be a famous athlete
and he would open camps
all across the country
free ones
for boys like him
where they could run
and play
and be free
and have no worries.

And that is still
what Max wants to be and do.

Max also reminds me
that when I was ten
I suddenly jumped off a swing
and said
Why are we here?

I remember that moment—
how I was swinging
and feeling so happy and free
watching the people in the park
all the mothers and fathers and
grandmas and grandpas and
children
going to and fro
but suddenly I felt shivery
alone and apart
dizzy from seeing all those people
and multiplying them by all the people
in all the towns and cities
in the world

and I jumped from the swing
with my urgent question:
Why are we here?

In the park? Max asked.

No! I shouted.
*Why are we here
on this earth?*

Max scowled at me.
I don't know, do I?
he said.

Am I supposed to do something
important?
It doesn't seem enough
to merely take up space
on this planet
in this country
in this state
in this town
in this family.

I know why Max wants to be
a famous athlete
but I do not yet know
what I should be
or
do.

QUESTIONS

When I ask Max why he hates our town
he shrugs
aims his deep gray eyes at me
then turns and sweeps his arm
through the air
as if he has waved it over the whole town
and he says
Too small.
Always the same.
I want to see what is out there—
and he stands on tiptoe
as if he could see over the tops
of the trees
to the rest of the world.

I don't understand Max.
The town seems huge to me
and never the same
everything changes:
the light, the smells, the sounds

and people coming and going
and growing bigger and older.

When Max says he will open camps
for *boys like him*
I ask him what kind of boy that is
and he aims his eyes at me again
and keeps them there
and keeps them there
and keeps them there
as he lifts one hand
to remove a leaf from my hair
and he says
Boys with nothing.

And he will not stand still for my reply.
He is already off and running
while I am wondering if I am part
of
the
nothing.

FEARS AND LOVES

My teacher, Mr. Welling, asked us
to make a list of things we fear.

I did not want to do it
my mind would not go there

until Mr. Welling said that after
we made our list of things we fear
we would make a list of things we love.

Things I Fear:

I am afraid of war
of shootings and murders

of other people killing our people
because our people killed their people
because their people killed our people
on and on
until maybe nobody will be left.

I am afraid of dying
and of my family dying

of disappearing
and not knowing
that you have disappeared
or being left alone
with no one to love you.

Things I Love:

I love running

out in the air
smelling the trees and grass
feeling the wind on my face
and the ground on my feet.

I love drawing

because it feels like running
in your mind
and on a blank page
a picture appears
straight out of your mind
a phantom treasure.

I love laughing

and hearing people laugh
because the sound of it
is rolling and free and full.

I love many many things

which sound too sappy
to write about.

Later, I hear others talking about
their fears and loves.

Some fear:
algebra and tests
essays and reports.

I am not good at these things
but I do not fear them
and I wonder if I am wrong.
I wonder if I am *supposed* to fear them.

Many of them love:
candy and television
weekends and sleeping.

I *like* these things
but I do not *love* them
and I wonder if I am *supposed* to love them

and I wonder if
I have done the assignment wrong

and when I look at my own list
of fears and loves
they seem too big

maybe not what the teacher had in mind

maybe not

but I am feeling stubborn
and so I do not erase them.

PUMPKIN ALIEN

My father speaks to the alien baby
aiming his words
at my mother's abdomen:

Hell-ooo, pumpkin alien baby
he says
how are you today?

He consults the baby book.
Let's see, pumpkin alien baby
you are nearly four months old
and you are this big—
he holds his hands
about four inches apart—
and you have fingers and toes
and are sprouting little tooth buds!

My father looks amazed
and my mother smiles
and I try to imagine
how this happens.

How does the alien baby
know how to grow fingers and toes
and little tooth buds?

I run my tongue over my own teeth
smooth and slippery
like polished stones.

I feel the slim space
between the front ones
a narrow doorway
for a sliver of air.

And I think about Grandpa's teeth
upstairs
in an old jelly jar
on a lace doily
beside his bed.

That night I dream
of an alien pumpkin
round and bright orange
with two rows of white teeth
clacking.

FRIED CHICKEN

Grandpa's room is next to mine
Annie! he calls. *Annie, Annie, Annie!*

I rush in
find him sitting in the blue chair.

A piece of paper rests in his lap
a pencil in his hand.

Annie, Annie!
How did I make fried chicken?

I would laugh except he is so earnest
in his question
a frown on his face
his eyes big and wide.

I can't remember how I made fried chicken!

I touch his hand and
tell him I will ask my mother

and Grandpa says
Hurry!

My mother is in the backyard
snipping the remains of lavender
from a frosted plant.

Smell this
she says
rubbing her fingers against the silvery leaves
and holding them to my nose.

It's a calming, soothing smell
softer than pine
gentler than roses.

I tell her about Grandpa's question
and my mother looks puzzled.

She says
But Grandpa made fried chicken
every single week for—for—maybe forty years!

How could he not remember how he made
fried chicken?

She wipes her hands on her jeans
and goes to Grandpa
where she explains exactly how
Grandpa used to make fried chicken
which is exactly how my mother
makes it now.

When she is done explaining
Grandpa says, *Again. I want to write it down.*
And so my mother repeats the process
and Grandpa writes it all down
and then says
Now how did you make those strawberries?

Strawberries? my mother says.

You know, you had them once
when your mom and I came over
and you were living in the yellow apartment—

But that was ten years ago!
my mother says
sitting on the bed beside
Grandpa's chair.

Grandpa waves his hand in the air.
They were in a little white bowl
strawberries
all cut up.
They were so good.
How did you make them?

My mother bites her lip.
I think I just cut them up.
I bought some strawberries
and I cut them up
and I put them in that bowl.
Maybe I sprinkled a little sugar on top.
That's all I did.

Grandpa nods.
Well, they were very good strawberries.

In my parents' room
I lift the miniature white T-shirt
from the basket that holds
a few little things for the baby.

The shirt seems infinitely small
too small for any living person
and I wonder if the alien baby
can think now
and if it can think
what does it think?

And what did I think
when I was small
and why did I forget?

And what else will I forget
when I grow older?

And if you forget
is it as if
it never happened?

Will none of the things
you saw or thought or dreamed
matter?

I fold the shirt and replace it in the basket
and I race down the steps
and out the door
and leap off the porch
into the chilly air

and run run run
over fallen leaves
yellow and brown
glazed with frost:
crunch, crunch, crunch.

SAVING

As I run past the church
I see Mrs. Cobber
and she calls to me
Annie-banany!
You going to clean my porch today?

Yes, Mrs. Cobber-obber
I'll be there later

and she salutes me
as I run up the hill.

In the summer, I mow Mrs. Cobber's lawn
with her old push mower
smelling of rust and oil.

It's a small lawn
easy to mow
and when you are done
it looks as if you have done
so much more

than walk back and forth
a few times with a little old mower
and Mrs. Cobber is so pleased
with the newly mown lawn.

She acts as if it is the best present
she has received in a long, long time.

In the fall, I rake her leaves
and in the winter tidy the garage
and the back porch
both filled with old creaky things:
benches and chairs and lamps
musty, dusty, and intriguing
(Who sat on this bench? This chair?
Who used this lamp?)

She pays me for these chores
even though my father said
I should do them for free
but Mrs. Cobber insisted
saying that I should save the money
for something special.

I know exactly what I will buy
and I am thinking of this when
I hear
Hey, Annie!

Hey, Max!

and we fall into step *thump-thump*
beside each other
my feet tingling from the frosted ground

and when we come to the bench
I suddenly feel shy with Max
aware of his long legs and long arms
and his breath floating into the air
and the silence seems full of something
I do not understand

and so I fill up the silence.

I tell him about the chores for Mrs. Cobber
and about the money
I am saving for something special

and I know Max gets paid for working at the diner
so I ask him if he is saving for something special

and he doesn't even blink
he wiggles his feet and says
Running shoes!

And he tells me he has to have them
for the track meets in the spring
because the coach won't let him run barefoot
and he has to get them in time
to break them in
and he hopes they work
because he has to win the meets
he *has to*

and then he tells me
again
for the nine millionth time
that I should join the girls' team
that I am stupid not to
and what am I afraid of

and I tell him I am not afraid
I do not want to join the team
I like to run by myself
or with Max

and he knows that I am mad
and so he asks me what I am saving for.

I tell him
about the box of charcoal pencils
soft and black as night
and colored pencils
with every pastel color
and the paper
thick and white
on which you can draw
whatever you want

and he nods
as if he understands how much I want
the pencils and paper
and how they are not ordinary ones
but special ones

and I like this about Max
that I do not have to explain

but then as we turn to run back
he says—
as if he cannot help himself—
But you really should join the team

and he takes off very fast

thump-thump, thump-thump

and my heart matches my steps

thump-thump, thump-thump

as I take off after him
forgetting the pencils and paper
and the team I do not want to join

forgetting everything
as I run.

FOOTNOTES

In school we are learning footnotes.[1]

It made me laugh to hear them called
FOOTnotes.

I pictured little notes on my feet
and could not stop giggling
as Mr. Welling tried to explain
why we needed to do footnotes[2]
and the exact, correct format

and we had to practice
everything exactly right
with the commas and the colons
in the right place.

He was very
par-tic-u-lar.

---

1. Like this.
2. To show where we found information, or sometimes to explain
something further.

And I liked getting everything
in the right place
and knowing there was a plan
for how to do it right

but then I could not get the footnotes
out of my mind
and started putting them everywhere—
on spelling tests
and on math homework—

and just about everywhere
where I wanted to add a little explanation
(which you do not normally have a chance to do
on tests or homework)

but I am not sure all of my teachers
appreciate the footnotes[3]

and now I am dreaming
in footnotes

---

3. One teacher wrote "Very amusing," but another put two angry
red question marks by each footnote.

which is a peculiar thing.

I dreamed of running past the barn
and in my head I saw a footnote
which said
Faded red barn
and when I passed the church
I saw a footnote
Old stone church
and on like that
footnotes for every little thing

and when I stopped at the red bench
and looked at the soles of my feet
all the little notes were printed there
in charcoal pencil

and somehow it pleased me
that the notes were there
imprinted on my feet—

footnotes.

THE SKELETON

Mom says she has a surprise
for me and Dad and Grandpa
and she makes us close our eyes
as she rummages in her purse
and then she says
Open!

She is holding what appears to be
a black-and-white photograph
of grayish stones on a deep black background.

Grandpa peers at the picture.
I think your camera needs fixing
he says.

My father is excited.
Is that—? Oh, man!
He inspects it, squints,
turns it upside down.

But where—? What—?

And then I remember that today
my mother was to have an ultrasound
and this must be a picture of the baby.

I snatch the photo from my father
and turn it this way and that
and my mother is laughing
and finally she says
Here, like this
and she turns the photograph
and traces the stones
This is the head
and this is the chest
and this is an arm
and this is a foot—

My father and Grandpa and I stare.
I wonder what they are thinking.
I am horrified.

It looks like a little skeleton head
and it does not look at all cute
and I am feeling so sorry for us
that we are going to have such a
frightening-looking baby.[4]

But my mother explains that we are
seeing the bones of the head
like an X-ray
and the shape of the head will change
and *of course* there is flesh on it
and the midwife said
that the heart and all the organs
were present and accounted for
and the baby looked perfect
in every way

which was some relief to my father
and Grandpa and me

and I surely hope the midwife is right.

---

4. An *extremely* frightening-looking baby.

My mother said that during the ultrasound
she could see
the arms moving
as if the baby were waving at her

and she said that the next appointment
was on a Saturday so that Dad and I
can go and hear the heartbeat—
the *heartbeat*!

A tear slipped down Grandpa's cheek.

Oh, you can come, too, Dad!
my mother said.
If you're up to it—

Grandpa nodded
as two more tears rolled down
his cheek.

Mom patted Grandpa's hand
and told me and my father that maybe

we should stop calling the baby
the alien baby
because it can hear
and we should
call it something nicer
so it will not get its
feelings hurt.

AN APPLE A DAY

Twice a week at school
we have art class with Miss Freely
in a room I'd like to live in
with its wide drawing tables
and easels
and paint-spattered floor
and smocks to cover your clothes
and drawers of paper
and pencils
and paints.

Yesterday Miss Freely said
we were going to draw apples.

Apples? Kaylee said.
Ordinary apples?

Miss Freely said
No apple is ordinary.
You'll see.

She let each of us choose an apple
from a basket:

mine was yellow with green freckles
on one side
and an orange blush on the other side.

Miss Freely asked us to study the apple.

Study the apple? Kaylee said.

Yes, Miss Freely said.
Study it as long as you want—
then draw one apple.

Only one? Kaylee said.

Only one today
Miss Freely said.
Take the apple home with you.
Draw this same apple each day.

Every day? Kaylee said.

Every single day?

Yes, Miss Freely said.

For how long? Kaylee asked.

For one hundred days, Miss Freely said.

One hundred days?
Draw one hundred pictures
of the same old apple? Kaylee asked.

Kaylee turned to me and said
That's an awful lot of drawings
of one apple.

It did seem like a lot.
I wondered if we would get tired
of drawing apples apples apples.

Miss Freely said
You can draw other things, too,
as usual

as long as you also draw an apple
each day.

Even days we don't have art class?
Kaylee asked.

Yes, Miss Freely said.
I think you will discover some interesting things.
I think you will discover the un-ordinary-ness
of an apple.

I couldn't wait to draw my first apple
and I knew exactly what I would draw it with:
colored pencils
and I knew exactly which paper I would use:
the smooth, white, thick paper
that lets the pencils glide over it.

Kaylee finished drawing her apple
in three minutes
and then she turned to drawing
what she really wanted to draw
which was a hat with feathers.

I studied my apple a long time.
It would be hard to get roundness
on the paper
so I looked in the books
on shading and perspective
to see how real artists
made round things look round
on the flat paper.

Miss Freely moved around the room
as she does
pausing to study each person's work
and answer questions and
offer suggestions like
*I wonder what would happen if you
tried a different color there?*

When she came to me she said
I do so like your line
which is something she has often
said to me
You have a distinct line
but I do not know exactly

what she means
because some of my lines
are straight and some are curved
and I do not see how my lines
are different from other people's lines.

Everyone else finished an apple drawing in class
but I only got the outline done
so Miss Freely let me take
four colored pencils home with me[5]
and everyone got to take their apples
and while I was running that afternoon
I thought about the apple
and thought about it
and thought about it
and when I got home
I drew apple number one.

It looked like an apple
which is the best I can say
for it.

---

5. Yellow, green, orange, brown.

It seemed a bit stiff
too much like a drawing of an apple
with none of the feeling of an apple.

HEARTBEAT

I expect to hear alien baby's
heartbeat
sound like mine
thump-THUMP, thump-THUMP

and as the midwife
lowers the Doppler
(which resembles a microphone)
to my mother's abdomen
my father and I stare
hard
as if staring will help us listen

and then—!
we hear a rushing sound
a-whoosh-a-whoosh-a-whoosh
very fast
as if the alien baby
must be running hard
a-whoosh-a-whoosh-a-whoosh-a-whoosh

the sound of a real heart
a baby heart
beating beating beating

a-whoosh-a-whoosh-a-whoosh
as our little baby rushes on

and I feel as if
this is my team
my mother and father and me
and the baby
a-whoosh-a-whoosh-a-whoosh

and Grandpa, too,
who wasn't feeling well enough
to join us, and who is at home
lying in his bed.

THE COACH

Today the girls' track team coach
stops me after lunch.

Max tells me you're quite a good runner
she says.

I don't know what to say to her.

You ought to try out for the track team
she says.

No, thank you.

She studies me and says
We need some good runners.

No, thank you.

She looks annoyed with me
but I can see that she is trying
not to show it.

She says
It's a lot of fun.

Why do people not listen when you say no?
Why do they think you are too stupid
or too young
to understand?
Why do they think you are too shy
to reply?
Why do they keep badgering you
until you will say yes?

I'm sorry, I say, *I just don't want to.*

She smiles her best smile and says
*Why don't you just come out to practice
one day and see what it's like?*

I want to punch her
but of course I will not punch her
because that is not a very civilized response.

I want to tell her that I've seen the practices
and nothing about them is appealing.

Everyone does the same warm-ups
the same sprints
the same cool-downs.

No one gets to run her heart out
no one runs barefoot
no one smiles.

No one can let her head go free.

And someone must win
and someone must lose

and always the winner looks proud
and the loser looks forlorn

and I can't understand why they all
would spoil
such a good thing
as running

but I know the coach will not leave me alone
until I say something that lets her win
and so I say
Okay, maybe I'll come watch.

But I don't mean it.

THE KICK

After dinner my mother eases herself
onto the sofa
and props up her feet.

Oh!
she says suddenly.
Oh! Oh!

Her eyes open so wide
and her mouth, too,
like a big round O.

Come here, Annie
she whispers
and so I sit beside her
as she places my hand
on her abdomen.

There!
A tiny nudge
a lump pushing against my hand

a soft *thump*
and then—there!
Another and another!

I pull my hand away.

The baby! my mother says.
That's the baby!

I put my hand back and wait
until—there! *Thump!*

And all evening all I can think about is
the thing
growing
and moving
inside my mother.

FLIP, FLIP, FLIP

I am in Grandpa's room
looking through the photo albums
with him.

We see Grandpa when he was my age
sitting on a picnic table
tanned legs swinging
arms spread wide
as if he wants to wrap up
the whole world.

It is hard to see my grandpa
in that boy
in that smooth skin
those skinny legs
that dark hair.

Grandpa studies this photo
a long time
as if he, too, wonders

how that young boy
turned into an old grandpa.

He flips through the pages
pausing to examine a young Grandma—
his new wife—
sitting on a riverbank
face tilted up to the sun.

On through the pages we go
witnessing their lives
flip, flip, flip
fast-forwarding through
my mother as a child
flip, flip, flip
until there's me
in Grandpa's arms
newly born
and Grandma is there, too.

They are smiling at me
as if I am a miracle baby.

Flip, flip, flip
I grow up
Grandma is gone
Grandpa's hair turns gray.

Flip, flip, flip.

PERSPECTIVE

Apples, apples, apples
thirty drawings of one apple.

The first ten looked pretty much alike
which was starting to bother me

and then one day when I was
out running
I glanced at budding branches overhead
and was thinking about spring
and the coming of new leaves
and how I usually see the undersides of leaves
and I would have to climb the trees
to see the leaves from the top

and I thought of my apple.

I could draw it from the top
looking down on it
and from underneath
looking up at it.

I could put it on its side!

And in the middle of thinking that
I hear
Hey, Annie!

Hey, Max!

And we run on round the bend
and past the birches[6]
and Max is running faster than usual

so I pick up my pace a little
down the hill
l-e-a-p-i-n-g over the creek

and I keep pace with him
up the hill
past the barn[7]

---

6. Tall and thin.
7. Faded red.

around the pasture
and Max is moving faster and faster
until we reach the red bench
where we stretch and flop

and Max checks his grandpa's pocket watch
and looks displeased

and says
You must've slowed me down, Annie.

I want to punch him
but I don't.

Instead I say
No, I think you *slowed* me *down, Max.*

He says, *Huh! Fat chance.*

And then he asks me
again again again
for the seven billionth time
if I am going to join the track team

and I tell him no

and he calls me a chicken

and I ask him why he thinks
not joining the team
makes me a chicken

and he says I am afraid
to lose
that I'm afraid
someone will be better
run faster

and I ask him why someone has to win
and someone has to lose
and why someone always has to
run
faster

and he looks at me as if I have
sprouted fangs
and he shakes his head

and says
You just don't get it, do you?

And I am thinking to myself
that he is the one
who does not get it
but already he is up and stretching
and he takes off running
and this time I let him go
ahead of me
faster faster faster
until he disappears round the bend

and I can go at my own pace
and let my head go free
and let the apples turn and roll
in my mind.

GRANDPA TALK

I am in Grandpa's room
preparing to draw my forty-fifth apple.

It perches on the glass shelf on his wall
and I am sitting on the floor
beneath it
studying it from the bottom.

Grandpa is sifting through
my fat folder of apples.

What an awful lot of apples!
he says.
They're making me hungry.

The apple on the glass shelf
does not look like an apple
from the bottom
and I don't know how I will draw it
and will it still be an apple
if it doesn't *look* like an apple?

While I am sitting there gazing at the apple
I tell Grandpa about the coach
asking me to try out for the track team
and about Max telling me the same
and about how the coach kept bugging me
and now the tryouts are over
and the coach does not even
look me in the eye

and then I tell him about Max saying
I am a chicken
and how I don't feel like a chicken
and how I love to run
but I don't want to run
in a herd

and I don't like watching people
worry about fast and faster and fastest
and about
winning and losing

and all the while I am talking
Grandpa is nodding, nodding
and finally he says
You stick to your guns, honey.

And I say
But they say I will regret it—

and Grandpa says
Do you think you will regret it?

And I say
*No—but they think I am wrong
that I can't know
what I will regret.*

And Grandpa says
*Wrong. Right. Regret.
When I stopped running races
everyone told me I was wrong
and everyone told me I would regret it.*

He is looking at the photo of himself
with the trophy.

I ask him
And did you regret it?

Grandpa shifts his gaze to my apple folder.
Not for one tiny minute
he says.

And I want him to say more
to tell me why he stopped running races
but he leans his head back against the chair
and closes his eyes
and falls asleep.

His face looks different in sleep
the muscles slack
the wrinkles smoothed.

Has that brown spot on his cheek
always been that large?
Has it always been the shape
of a pear?

I draw his profile:
the wide forehead
the unruly eyebrows
the noble nose
the downturned mouth.

Is he not happy in his sleep?

I draw the brown spot
and the dimpled chin.

I lie back on the floor
and close my eyes
and try to keep the image
of my grandpa's face
in my mind

and I dream
not of races
but of colored pencils
and charcoal pencils
and thick, white, smooth paper
and Grandpa's face.

MAD MAX

Hey, Annie-banany!
Mrs. Cobber calls as I run past the church
You going to cut my grass today?

Yes, Mrs. Cobber-obber
I'll be there later.

And I am happy to mow
Mrs. Cobber's lawn today
because then I will have enough money
to buy the charcoal pencils
and the colored pencils
and the white paper.

Hey, Max!

Hey, Annie—

Max looks angry
black mood all around him
and I do not even try to pick up my pace.
I let him surge ahead of me.

I can hear and feel his feet
pounding hard
thump-thump, thump-thump

and when I reach the bench
he is sitting there with his head hanging
between his legs
breathing hard.

I stretch and sit and tap his back.

What's the matter?
I ask.

Nothing. Everything.

I examine the soles of my feet
wishing there were words there
magic words to say to Max
but there is only dirt on my feet
and one lone pebble.

You get your shoes yet?
I ask.

I know the coach has been letting him
run barefoot for practices
but I know he has to have the shoes
for the first meet.

No, he says.

*You going to have time to get them
and break them in?*

He talks to the ground, angrily:
They cost so much money, Annie!

Can you borrow someone else's shoes?
I ask.

He doesn't answer.
I check out his feet
wondering if maybe my father's shoes
would fit him

although I know my father's tennis shoes
are not the kind that Max has in mind—
they are not stylish
or new or clean.

I have a little money
I hear myself saying
and I want to cut off my tongue
because I don't want to part with my money
but before I can say more
Max stands and says
No. Thank. You.

And he takes off running
back down the path
and I stay on the bench
secretly glad that he does not want my money
but profoundly sad that he seems
angry
with
me
and

I
do
not
know
why.

And then I wonder:
if I joined the team
would Max not be mad at me
and if I won the races
would Max not be mad at me?

But it does not seem a good reason
to join a team—
just so someone will not be mad at you.

THE BIRTHING CENTER

Today we visited the birthing center
where my mother will have the baby.

It is not a hospital[8] —
it looks like a house
and has offices downstairs
and bedrooms upstairs
where the babies will be born.

You can choose your room:
the Colonial, which has a four-poster bed
or the Modern, which is all sharp angles
or the Regency, which is extremely flouncy.

My mother has chosen the Colonial.

Next to each bedroom is a room
sheltering a blue whirlpool tub
and on the other side of the bedroom

---

8. My mother does not like hospitals.

is a bathroom
and across from that is an office
with an incubator and scales
and scary-looking equipment.

Only women work here
most of them are midwives
and they will bring the baby
into the world

and if there is a problem[9]
there is a hospital five minutes away.

My mother loved the birthing center
but my father looked a little worried
and on the way home he asked my mother
again if she was absolutely sure
that this is where she wanted
to have the baby

9. I am not wanting to think about problems.

and she said yes
and she reminded him that
at the birthing center
both he and I
could be present
for the whole birth.

We would not miss one single moment.

My father cleared his throat
and tried to smile
because I think he really wants to be there
and to be a good husband and father
but he feels a little queasy about it, too

and me, I am so proud that I can be there
it makes me feel grown up
but I am also a little queasy

because I do not want to see my mother
in pain
and I do not know if I can stay calm

which is what the midwives say that
we will need to be.

We have to study the coaching manuals
to know how to help my mother breathe
and we have to watch the videos
to know what to expect

and the birth of the alien baby
is starting to seem more real
and I am going to be there
and I will have a sister or brother
and I will not be afraid.[10]

---

10. I hope.

APPLE

I have been feeling so proud
that I have not lost my apple.

Most people are on their third or fourth
apple by now
but I've been hoping to keep mine
right up until the one hundredth
drawing.

Its skin has not been looking so shiny
lately
and sometimes it seems that it has
shrunk
but still it is MY apple

completely different
from anyone else's apple
which came as a surprise to me.

Sometimes I can stare at one tiny patch
of my apple

for the longest time
and the more I study it
the more I see in that one little patch:
the smallest indentations
multiple colors
flecks and spots—
a miniature landscape.

I thought that the apple
would be easier to draw each day
but it is harder
trying to capture all those
colors and flecks and spots.

When I was running today
and thinking about the apple
I felt as if I was full of that apple
and I *knew* the apple[11]

---

11. I know this sounds peculiar.

and I couldn't wait to get home
to draw it

but
I
could
not
find
my
apple.

I always leave it in the same place
on my windowsill
but I searched my whole room
and then the rest of the house
and then I peeked into Grandpa's room.

He was lying on the bed
asleep
and I was about to close the door again
when I saw it—
my apple—
on his nightstand

with
one
bite
taken
out
of
it.

THE BITE

It was very good
Grandpa says
as I snatch the apple
from his nightstand
but I didn't want to eat any more.
I was saving it for later.

I feel sad for my poor bitten apple
but I put it back on the nightstand
and as I am leaving the room
I get an idea:
I will draw the apple
with a bite out of it
and then I will draw the apple
with two bites out of it
and on and on
a diminishing apple
vanishing
until
there
is

just

a

core

remaining

and something else I know instantly:
that I will not need to look at the apple[12] —
that I can draw
the apple that's in my mind.

12. Which will probably already have vanished into my grandpa
anyway.

LINES

On the days we have art class
Miss Freely shows us how to use
different mediums
pen and ink
charcoal
pastels
acrylics.

I have drawn my apple
with each of them
and my favorites are
the pen and ink
and the chalky pastel ones.

Miss Freely asked us each to choose
our ten favorite apple drawings
so far
and she has posted these
all around the room
hundreds of apples

apples apples apples
everywhere.

I walk round and round
the room
looking at all the different apples
and I spot one
which looks like a hat
an apple hat
so I know it must be Kaylee's.

At first I think I will not find mine
among all the hundreds of apples
but they jump out at me
and I know them instantly
as mine.

I know my line

and now I can see what Miss Freely
says about line

how you can see the difference
among the drawings.

Miss Freely is looking through
the rest of my folder
sixty apples
plus the ten on the wall
seventy days
seventy apples.

She closes the folder
and holds it to her chest
and pats the folder
once
twice

and then she moves on
to another student's folder

and I am wondering
what she thinks

and suddenly I think
that I will be sad
when I draw the
one hundredth apple

because it will be
the apple core

and because now I know
that there is still so much more
to learn about apples.

FORBIDDEN WORDS

Mr. Welling put a list of forbidden words
on the board today.
He says we use these words too much
and they are empty words and phrases
and we should try to talk and to write
without using them.

Here is his list:

very
like
ya know?
uh
well
stuff
yeah

Kaylee raised her hand and said
Well, what—

Mr. Welling tapped the board
next to the word *well*.

Kaylee started again
Like, ya know—

Mr. Welling tapped the board
at *like* and *ya know*.

Kaylee was getting angry.

What I am trying to ask—

She paused, listening to herself
pleased that she'd managed
not to say any forbidden words
before she moved on.

is, like—wait! No! Don't tap!
What I am trying to ask—

She paused again, thinking.

is—is—well, crud—no, not well—

Most of us were laughing
we couldn't help it
and Kaylee turned to us and said
If you think it is so easy, you try it!

And so other people tried to speak
but each of us could barely ask
a single question
or make a single comment
without using at least one
of the forbidden words.

It was very—oops, no, not very—
it was *extremely* amusing.

It is easier in writing to avoid
the forbidden words
but I see that I do use
very
a lot.[13]

_____

13. A *very very very* lot.

SHOELESS

After school I see Max at the track
being scolded by his coach
who is holding a pair of running shoes
worn and beaten
waving them in front of Max.

I cannot hear the coach's words
but I figure he is trying to get Max
proud Max
to take the used shoes.

Max stands with his arms crossed
defiant
scowling

and I am thinking he should not be
so proud
when I see the girls' coach
coming toward me.

She says
I saw you run yesterday, Annie
up near the stone church—
that was you, wasn't it?

I say, *Maybe.*

She says, *You have a fine stride—*

I cross my arms
like Max.

What is it you're afraid of?
she asks.

I do so want to punch her[14]
because there is something about her
some poking, prying, pushy thing
that engulfs me
but I do not punch her
instead I say

---

14. Very very very much.

I am not afraid.
I love to run
but I love to run by myself.

She studies me
disbelieving
a little scornful
as if I am hiding something
or lying to her
and then she smiles
a thin little smile
and says
You might enjoy being
part of a team.

And now I *really* want to slug her[15]
because I have heard this before
from other coaches
who think that if you don't
want to be
part of a team

---

15. I want to slug her very very much.

there is something wrong with you—
perhaps you are a future
ax murderer

and so I know I have to find
some little thing
to let her win
and so I say
Yes, ma'am
maybe I would enjoy being
part of a team—
someday. [16]

And so, victorious,
she says
Well, [17] *you think about it*
and let me know when
you're ready.

---

16. And maybe I wouldn't.
17. Forbidden word.

And I say
Yes, ma'am
I will.

And she says
Because, ya know, [18]
you shouldn't waste
a gift.

And I say
Yes, ma'am.

And when I get home
I fling off my shoes
and flee for the path
and I run
hard and fast
on the soft spring ground
so that I barely see Max
zoom from out of the trees

Hey, Annie!

---

18. Forbidden words.

but I don't answer
because my chest is too tight

and we run fast and faster
and today I want to beat Max
to the bench
and I fly down the hill

f-l-y over the creek
zoom up the path.

We are neck and neck
and we are breathing hard
and I soar over the grass

thump-thump, thump-thump.

I feel as if I am weightless
and free
as I lunge for the bench
reaching it one slim second
before
Max

and we hunch over
huffing and puffing
and he says
That's a little better pace, Annie

and I slug him hard

and turn and fly for home
fast and faster and fastest

and all the way
I am apologizing
to the air
to the sky
for not wanting
to waste a gift
but knowing
that I am right
and knowing
that I do not like
to be wrong
which is probably
a serious character flaw.

A GIFT

I am sorry
for punching Max

and so I take my lawn-mowing money
and place it in an envelope
and write Max's name on it
using my left hand
to disguise my handwriting

and I slip it in through
the vents of his locker

and hope that he will have enough
to buy his shoes
and be part of a team
and win his race.

PUMPKIN BABY

We are calling the alien baby
the pumpkin baby now
partly because my mother
looks as if she is carrying a pumpkin
in there.

Pumpkin baby is eight months old
more than a foot long
and weighs about five pounds.

It can hiccup and suck its thumbs
and open its eyes.

Mom is practicing her breathing
and Dad and I are coaching her.
We have to say things like
Relax your forehead
relax your arms
breathe in
breathe out.

We have seen the birthing videos
which gave me nightmares
because they show *everything*
and it looks hard and painful
for both the mother and the baby
and a million things can go wrong

but my mother says that
a million things can go right, too
and that a billion things
have already gone right
to enable our pumpkin baby
to have eyes and ears and toes
and heart and liver and lungs
and
heartbeat
a-whoosh-a-whoosh-a-whoosh.

And now I am not dreaming
of baby mice or rabbits or horses.
I dream of real babies.

Last night I dreamed
of a baby no bigger than my hand
and I was watching it
but I lost it
and I was frantic
searching everywhere
until finally I found it
behind the radiator
where it had got too hot
and the baby was
melting
melting
melting.

And I don't understand
why I can't dream
of perfect babies
with all their fingers
and all their toes
and a perfect
perfect
sister.[19]

19. Who does not lose or melt the baby.

TREASURE OF WORDS

Now Mr. Welling is on a crusade
about using the thesaurus
to help us find synonyms
because our vocabularies
are needing some help
he says.

He is exceedingly big on the thesaurus.
It's a treasure of words
he says.
Thrilling! Sensational! Exhilarating!

I try to use it
but it stops my mind
and I forget where I am going
but Mr. Welling says
to *soar* ahead and write the first draft
fast
as I usually do
and then later go back and
plumb

the thesaurus
for more thrilling
sensational
exhilarating
words.

I am *endeavoring*
to do so
but sometimes
the *consequences*
make me *resonate*
rather *abnormal*

but I did *perceive*
some *compelling*
revelations.

I *detected* a *quantity* of synonyms
for angry—
now when I run into the girls' track coach

I can say that she makes me
aggravated
annoyed
antagonized
bitter
displeased
enraged
exasperated
furious
heated
hot
incensed
indignant
infuriated
irate
irritated
mad
outraged
passionate
and
raging.

THE STRANGER

Annie! Annie! Grandpa calls.

He sounds frightened.

I find him huddled in his blue chair
his arms hugging his chest.

What is it, Grandpa?
What's wrong?

He points to the photo on the wall
the one of him standing with the trophy.

Who is that boy?
Grandpa asks.
He's staring at me!

Grandpa, that's you.

Grandpa looks at the photo
suspiciously.

Well, he says, *he's* bothering *me!*

Do you want me to take him away?
I ask.

Grandpa's chin quivers.
He nods.

I remove the photo from the wall
and take it to my room
and then I return to Grandpa
and say
Is that better?

He studies the blank space on the wall
his chin still quivering.
He looks small and frightened
like a child.

He nods slowly.
He was bothering me so much
Grandpa says.

I sit on the bed beside Grandpa.
Why? I ask. *What was he doing?*

Grandpa seems a little braver
now that the photo is gone.

He leans toward me and whispers
He wouldn't stop staring at me!

I do not like to see my grandpa like this.
Always he was so busy
so wise
so comforting.
Always he was the grandpa
the one who knew everything
the one who would laugh with me
and run with me.

Grandpa looks around the room
as if checking to see if anyone is listening
and then he says
Go ask him why he was staring at me.

And because my grandpa is so serious
I leave the room and go into mine
and I say, aloud
Why were you staring at my grandpa?
and I listen for the photo's response
and return to Grandpa and say
He was staring at you because
he likes you.

Pff! Grandpa spurts
but a grin has appeared on his face
and he seems flattered and boyish.

I say
Do you want me to bring him back?

Grandpa thinks a minute
considering
and then he says
No. Not right now.
Maybe he can come back tomorrow.

SHOES

Thump-thump, thump-thump
running up the path
in the balmy air
full of flowery smells
and zinging bees.

Hey, Annie-banany!
You going to cut my grass today?

Yes, Mrs. Cobber-obber
I'll be there later

and she salutes me
as I think about starting over
saving money
for the pencils and paper
or maybe the chalky pastels.

Hey, Annie!

Hey, Max!

He stumbles, trips
regains his stride.

Hey, you got your shoes!
I say
staring down at the new white
enormous shoes.

Yeah! he says
his chin jutting out as if
it is leading him along the trail.

He stumbles, trips, scowls.
Not used to them yet
he says.
Big race Friday.
Gotta beat these things into shape by then.

L-e-a-p over the creek
up the hill

proud of my secret gift to Max[20]
feeling good running free.

You going to be there?
he asks.

I stumble, trip
surprised by his question
by the intensity in his voice
as if it matters to him
that I be at the race.

Where? I say
composing myself as best I can.
The race?

Of course the race!
You going to watch me win?

I don't want to think about it.
I don't want to see him in the herd
and what if he doesn't win?

---

20. But also a little annoyed that he hasn't even *mentioned* the
anonymous donor.

He reaches out, taps my arm.
You'd better be there, Annie.

Yeah, I say, feeling
confused
baffled
bewildered
disarranged
discomposed
disoriented
embarrassed
flustered
mortified
muddled
and
perplexed.[21]

---

21. Courtesy of the thesaurus.

PRESENTS

On Grandpa's birthday I give him
a booklet I've made:
twenty drawings of Grandpa.

Some are small, pieces of the whole:
an eye
a hand
a foot
a mouth.

Some are large, the parts assembled:
asleep on the bed
sitting in the blue chair
eating my apple.

And one, my favorite, at the end:
Grandpa as a boy
running
on a path through the woods.

Grandpa smiles at each drawing
touching them
lingering over them

and when he is finished
he hugs me to him
and says
You've been spying on me!

He says he has a present
for me, too.

He wants me to know where it is
and what it is
but I am not to open it
until he kicks the bucket.

I cannot bear to hear him joke
about kicking the bucket
and maybe he senses this
because he says

You know I would stay here forever
if I could, don't you?

He asks me to open a drawer
in his desk
and to find a narrow yellow box.

That's for you
he says
for . . . later.

There are letters inside.

Thirteen, he says.
One written the day you were born
and one written on each of your birthdays.

The envelopes are a rainbow of colors:
yellow, blue, pink, violet
and around each is a white ribbon.

I want to open them now
I want to read every one

but I know he doesn't want me to—
not now.

I pull a quilt up to his chin
and kiss his forehead
and feel as if I should hold him
but I don't know how to do it.

THE RACE

After school, I decide I'll go to the race
then I decide I won't
then I will
then I won't.

I slip to the track
stand off to the side.

The herds are all there
bouncing
stretching
pacing
jogging.

Boys will go first
then the girls.

I wish Max didn't want this so much
and I feel odd—
as if in order to wish him well
I have to hope that others do badly—

and I find myself not wanting
to be a part of this.

The air is steamy
heavy with expectation.
A grasshopper leaps across my foot
and seconds later
another grasshopper follows.

I spot Max in his herd
in his own world
stretching
bouncing
shaking his hands loose
rolling his head from side to side.

I pace around the field
as the first group sets off:

starter horn
whistles
cheers.

Can't bear to see the winner
and the losers.

Pace pace pace
until
Max's herd is up
horn blares
Max flies away
pumping hard
finding his stride.

Round the bend now
he's starting to relax
looking good
head up
chin out
arms close in

and then he stumbles, trips

and I freeze
like a statue on the grass
mouth open

hand stretched toward Max
as if I could push him
to the finish line.

And in my frozen moment
Max has kicked off his shoes
and I think, *Yay, Max!*

He's pumping his arms
in the middle of his herd
but he's lost ground.

Hey, Annie, Annie, Annie!

It's Mrs. Cobber-obber.

*Annie, Annie, Annie
come quick!
Your mama's baby's coming!*

For a moment, I am frozen again
unable to move
watching Max overtake one runner

and another
and another

and I see the winner
cross the finish line
and it is not Max.

I wonder how he feels
and want to see his face
but Mrs. Cobber is pulling at my sleeve
and off I go with her—

the baby is coming!

FLURRY

Dad is carrying Mom's suitcase to the car
trying to look calm.
Mom is in the kitchen
leaning against the counter
pff, pff, pff
breathing hard.

Pff, pff, pff
Oh, Annie, I'm glad
pff, pff, pff
you made it
pff, pff, pff.

Run check on Grandpa
pff, pff, pff
see if he'll be okay with Mrs. Cobber
pff, pff, pff.

Grandpa is sitting in his blue chair
eyeing Mrs. Cobber warily
as she pulls up a chair across from him.

Annie, who is this woman?
he asks me.

Grandpa, you know her—
that's Mrs. Cobber
and she's going to stay with you
while I go with Mom—
she's having the baby!

A hint of recognition in Grandpa's eyes.
Yes, he says to Mrs. Cobber
we're having a baby today!

Mrs. Cobber pulls a deck of cards
from her pocket.
Do you like cards?
she asks Grandpa.

Yes, he says, *I do*
and then he turns to me
and says

too loudly
Tell her not to talk too much, okay?

Mrs. Cobber smiles.
Don't you worry
she says.
I am a woman of few words.

Okay, then
Grandpa says

and I leave them there

and race downstairs

and Mom is making her way
to the front door
pff, pff, pff.

Dad and I help her down the steps
and off we go

and my eyes are glued to my mother
whose eyes are closed
and my dad is trying to drive
while glancing from the road to my mother
back and forth

and it's all happening too fast
and I can't think
and I'm excited
and I'm terrified.

And what about Max?
Is he in his black mood
throwing his shoes in the river?

LABOR

The manuals have taught me
that it can take a long, long time
for a baby to be born
and so we have brought
books and magazines and playing cards
and enough food for ten people

but when the midwife examines my mother
she says
Hmm. You're pretty far along already.

My mom attempts a weak smile.

The midwife ushers her straight to
the whirlpool tub.
I hear her get in and sigh heavily.
Dad is with her.

I look around the Colonial room:
at the bed with its blue sheets
the blue-curtained windows

the soft lighting
and I feel the quietness of the room
the readiness for the baby.

I hear Dad saying:
Breathe in, breathe out
relax your brow
breathe in, breathe out.

I sit on the blue bed
surprised at how I feel
as if I am immersed in the water, too
and there is a rhythm to living and breathing
and birthing a baby

and one moment I feel alone
and apart
no longer my mother's only child
no longer a center of her world

and the next moment I feel
completely bound to my mother
as if I am *her*
or she is *me*
and I feel as if I will bawl like a baby.

Breathe in, breathe out
relax your brow.

I think of all the mothers
all over the world
and all the babies

and I was one of those babies
and this is my mother

and maybe this will be me one day

breathing in, breathing out.

PUSHING

Labor is the right word:
it is work, hard work
for the mother's body

but the whirlpool tub has helped
and when Mom is resettled in the bed
the midwife says
Okay, now we push.

My mother seems to be in a trance
somewhere else
and we have to call to her
bring her back from far away
so that she can push, pause, push.

I am on one side of her
Dad on the other.
Mom is gripping our hands[22]
but I am not really sure

---

22. Very very very tightly.

that she knows we are there
so deep in her trance is she.

When the midwife announces
that she sees the baby's head
my father and I stare at each other
The head! The head of the baby!

This seems astounding
even though it is what we all have been
preparing for.

An assistant enters and checks
the baby's heart rate
whispers to the midwife
and there is new urgency now
as the midwife says
I want you to push NOW
I want you to push very strongly NOW
We have to get this baby out NOW!

And I feel everything crumbling
so fragile and tentative and precarious

but we must give calm to my mother
and so we mop her brow
and grip her hands and tell her
she is doing great
and the baby is coming
and *Push, push NOW!*

The midwife's face is sober, serious
her hands working rapidly
her voice tight, saying
something about the shoulder
and something about pushing

but my mother seems not to hear
and we have to speak loudly to her
Push, push NOW!

The baby comes out
just like that
in a sudden rush
into the midwife's gloved hands

and the next instant
the baby is lying there
on the blue sheet
and the baby is not moving.

ETERNITY

My father and I stare at the baby
grayish and motionless.

We avert our eyes, turn to my mother
whose face is full of expectancy.
The baby's out! I say
trying to sound more hopeful than I feel.

I feel as if I have to *will* the baby to live:
live, live, live
breathe, breathe, breathe.

The midwife and the assistant
work rapidly
clearing the baby's nose and mouth
and I am thinking
How can the baby not be alive
when it was moving
and its heart was beating
just minutes ago?
And how can all of this—

all the morning sickness and the backaches
and the growing belly
and the dreaming
and the labor
and the pushing—
how could it NOT all end with a
living, breathing baby?
How could we bear it?

The midwife says
Just a couple puffs of oxygen
is all we need.
Her voice sounds strained.

I see the oxygen tube
hear a soft noise
a *pfft, pfft*
as the air goes into the baby
and maybe it has only been a minute
since the baby came out
but it seems as if it has been an eternity
as if it has been hours and a lifetime.

I turn to my mother
not wanting to betray my fear
but needing to see her face
and as I do so
we all hear
Wahh, wahh
and there is the baby
squirming
and crying
and breathing

and the relief rustles
through the room—
you can see it, feel it, hear it.

Everyone bursts into tears
mother, father, me, midwife

and it is only then that my father and I
look again at the baby
to see whether it is a boy or a girl

and my father proudly announces to my mother
that they have a son
and I have a brother.

The midwife lifts the baby to my mother's chest
and my mother says
Oh, oh, oh, oh, oh
and she is laughing and crying
and I cannot take my eyes off the baby
whose own eyes are open
and who gazes directly into my mother's eyes.

The baby has perfect hands and feet and
fingers and toes and ears
and eyes and nose
(and it is a *human* baby
which is a great relief)

and I know that everyone else says this
but I don't know how else to say it:
it is a *miracle*—
a marvel—
an astonishing

astounding
fabulous
incredible
phenomenal
prodigious
stupendous
wondrous
miracle.

WATCHING

I phone Grandpa and tell him the news.
He cries a little
and then he says
Everyone okay? Your mom? The baby?
Your dad? You?

Yes, yes, yes, we're all okay.

It is the middle of the dark night
and Mom has nursed the baby
and now she and my dad are asleep
on the bed
and I am sitting in the overstuffed chair
in the calm blue room
holding my new brother.

All I can do is stare at him
as he sleeps.
I stare hard and listen
to be sure he is breathing
and I touch his small fingers

so perfect and long
and I touch his cheek so warm so soft

and I whisper to him:
I tell him he is a miracle
and that he is perfect in every way
and that we will love him and take care of him
always.

The midwife says that after my mom
gets a good sleep
and eats a good meal
we can all go home.

This is frightening
because it seems too soon
and the baby seems so fragile
and what if we don't know what to do
and what if there is an emergency?
What if he stops breathing
and needs more puffs of air?

INFINITELY JOEY

I do not know how babies—
so small, so fragile—
ever grow up—
how their hearts can beat strongly enough
and how they continue to breathe
and how they do not perish
from the endless dangers
all around:

what if someone drops him?
what if he doesn't eat?
what if he gets sick?

Our baby relies on us for everything:
warmth and food and clothing
protection and safety
and love.
He *needs* us to love him
and it makes me worry
about all the babies in the world

who might not be warm or fed
or protected or loved.

He seems infinitely delicate
and yet infinitely whole
already a person.

I stare at him for hours
wondering who he *is*

and what he will look like
as he grows
and what he will think and do.

The answers seem all bound up
in the small bundle of this baby
answers already there
waiting to unfurl
like a bud on a tree.

I wish that every baby everywhere
could land in a family
that wanted that baby
as much as we want ours.

I do not know how I—
once a baby this small—
became *me*

nor how my mother or father
or grandfather or Max
all once so small and fragile
became who they are

nor if—
even when we were all alien babies—
if we already were
so much of who we are.

The baby will not remember
that we change his diapers
a thousand, thousand times
nor that we sing to him

and hold him
and bathe him
and mop his blurps

just as I do not remember
my parents and my grandparents
doing these many small things for me.

This bundle is our baby
my brother.

This is Joey.

SLEEPING

Grandpa is lying on his bed
with the baby asleep on his chest
the two of them curled together
peacefully.

I lie beside them
sneaking one arm over them
making sure they are both breathing
thump-THUMP, thump-THUMP
and I feel infinitely happy
that this miracle baby
has come to us
and infinitely
infinitely
infinitely
sad
that my grandpa

does not have a whole
long
life
ahead
of
him.

A SECRET

I am running
down the path
up the hill.

Hey, Annie-banany! How's that baby?

Fine, Mrs. Cobber-obber! Perfect!

It feels so good to run
to fill up with air
where everything looks green and lush
everything in harmony.

Hey, Annie—

Max's voice is sour
not in harmony.

Hey, Max—

He runs with his head down
not speaking
sullen
tense.

I can't help myself:
We have a new baby!
It's a boy and his name is Joseph—Joey—
after my grandpa—
and he is beautiful and—

That's great, just great
Max mutters
interrupting me
chopping off my words
letting them fall onto the path
like dead leaves.

I take it you didn't see the race?
he asks.

I try to tell him that I was there
but was called away by Mrs. Cobber
because the baby was coming,
but he chops my words again:
Well, I didn't win.

He says it roughly
accusingly
as if it was my fault.

We run past the birches[23]
l-e-a-p over the creek
past the barn[24]
round the pasture.

We reach the bench
and stretch and flop
and I check the soles of my feet
searching for words
but there is still no help on my feet

---

23. Tall and thin, bursting with leaves.
24. Newly painted, bright red!

and finally I say
Did you feel bad?

His answer is a hiss:
Yessss!
Was I supposed to feel good*?*

It was only one race—
I try, but he chop-chops my words.

I had to win that race.
I had *to.*

I don't ask why.

We start back down the path
retracing our steps
black black black
Max-mood all around us

but when we reach the place
where we normally part

I grab his arm
and ask him to come with me.

He tries to pull away.
You want me to see the baby,
don't you?
I don't want to see the—

But I chop his words
chop-chop:
Max, you are coming with me.
This will only take five minutes
and you are not going to argue with me.

I pull him along
until I feel him give in
and when we reach our house
I tug him inside and upstairs
where Mom is leaning in the doorway
of Grandpa's room
smiling at Grandpa
sitting in his chair
with the baby curled against his chest.

Grandpa is humming a little melody
to the baby
and when he sees us
he pulls the baby a little closer
to him.

It's okay, Grandpa, this is Max.
Remember Max?

Grandpa studies him a moment
and then nods
and releases the baby
to my open arms.

As I offer the baby to Max
he takes one step backward
but I nudge the baby into Max's arms.

To my surprise
Max takes the baby gently
and cradles him in his arms
as if he has been holding babies
all his life.

He strokes baby Joey's cheek
and then glances round the room.

He spies the photograph of Grandpa
with his trophy.

It is the photograph which Grandpa
had asked me to take away
but which, I see, he has retrieved.

Max asks Grandpa about the photograph
and they talk of races and running
and I leave them alone
while I shower and change
and when I return

Grandpa has baby Joey again
and Max is holding a box
and thanking my grandpa.

Outside, Max says that Grandpa
gave him a gift
and told him a secret about running.

He opens the box and shows me the gift:
Grandpa's running shoes
sixty years old.

Lucky shoes! Max says.

They are worn and stained
and they look nothing like
the new shoes that Max bought.

I feel a little jealous that Grandpa
has given these shoes to Max
and not to me.

I ask Max what the secret was
and Max says
I can't tell you, can I?
It's a secret.

But he smiles and his black mood is gone
and he waves as he trots off down the road
cradling his lucky shoes
and his secret.

Upstairs, I take baby Joey from Grandpa
and press the warm bundle to me
and Grandpa says
You're wondering why I gave him the shoes,
aren't you?

Yes.

Honey, you like to run barefoot
he says
and you don't need those old smelly shoes.

I ask him about the secret he told Max.

Honey, he says, *you already know the secret.*

Baby Joey wakes, squirms, cries
and Grandpa whispers to him:
Run for the pleasure of running.
It's a secret, baby.

THE PACKAGE

Tied to my locker is a plastic bag
and taped to the bag is a yellow card
with my name scrawled in awkward letters
like a child's printing.

Inside the bag:
a dozen colored pencils
and
smooth, thick, white paper.

A gift!
An anonymous gift!

But I know who it's from.

After school, I run run run—

Hey, Annie!

Hey, Max!

And on we go
as we always do
up and down the hills
o-v-e-r the creek

and at the bench I mention[25]
the extraordinary gift
the anonymous gift

and I turn to Max
who turns to me
and
we do not blink
until he says
Ready to run back?

And I say
Ready.

---

25. Casually.

And off we go
breathing in
breathing out
thump-thump, thump-thump

and I think it odd
but right
that this is the way we talk
run run run
thump-thump, thump-thump.

YUM BOY

On the last day of school
as Kaylee and I are cleaning out our lockers
we overhear two older girls
talking about Max:

He's so, I don't know, like, [26] *mysterious!*

Yeah, [27] *and so cute, so* yum*!*

I laugh, not sure why.

Kaylee asks me if I like Max.

Sure, I say.

But, like, ya know [28]
Kaylee persists
like, [29] *do you* really *like him?*

---

26. Forbidden word.
27. Ditto.
28. Ditto.
29. Ditto.

I shrug
just like Max does
and I think about moody Max
and running Max
and the Max who removes a leaf
from my hair
and the Max who pesters me
and the Max who holds Joey
and the Max who wants secrets
and lucky shoes
and who has big dreams

and I don't know how to answer Kaylee
because I do like Max
all of Max
even the moods and the pestering

but I am not ready
yet
to think of him

the way the other girls
are thinking of him

and I want him to stay Max
my same moody Max
and I want him to run with me
for a little longer.

ONE HUNDRED APPLES

Grandpa and baby Joey and I
are looking through my apple folder.
Grandpa points out his favorites
as Joey gazes wisely
as if he understands
what he is seeing.

Grandpa reaches the ninety-ninth apple:
a slim core
eaten away
a narrow indented column
with a dignified but bent stem
and pale flesh
browning at the edges.

As Grandpa turns the page
to the one hundredth apple
I hear a small intake of breath.

He takes the baby's finger
and together they trace
the drawing:

a small shiny brown seed
tear shaped
elegant
both old and new
silent
and
full
of
secrets.